There's a lot more to math than numbers and sums.
It's an important language that helps us describe, explore, and
explain the world we live in. So the earlier children develop
an appreciation and understanding of math, the better.

We use math all the time—when we shop or travel from one
place to another, for example. Even when we fill the kettle to make
hot chocolate, we are estimating and judging quantities.
Many games and puzzles involve math. So do stories
and poems, often in imaginative and interesting ways.

Math Together is a collection of high-quality picture books
designed to introduce children, simply and enjoyably, to basic
mathematical ideas—from counting and measuring to pattern and
probability. By listening to the stories and rhymes, talking about
them, and asking questions, children will gain the confidence
to try out the mathematical ideas for themselves—
an important step in their numeracy development.

You don't have to be a mathematician to help your child
learn math. Just as by reading aloud you play a vital role in their
literacy development, so by sharing the **Math Together** books
with your child, you will play an important part in developing their
understanding of mathematics. To help you, each book has detailed
notes at the back, explaining the mathematical ideas that it
introduces, with suggestions for related activities.

With **Math Together**, you can count on doing
the very best for your child.

For Milo
E. B.

For Helen Craig
D. P.

Text copyright © 1993 by Eileen Browne
Illustrations copyright © 1993 by David Parkins
Notes for parents copyright © 1999 by Jeannie Billington and Grace Cook

First U.S. edition in this form 2000

Library of Congress Catalog Card Number 92-53134

ISBN 0-7636-0958-7

2 4 6 8 10 9 7 5 3 1

Printed in Malaysia

This book was typeset in Goudy.
The illustrations were done in pen and ink and watercolor.

Candlewick Press
2067 Massachusetts Avenue
Cambridge, Massachusetts 02140

No Problem

Eileen Browne • David Parkins

CANDLEWICK PRESS
CAMBRIDGE, MASSACHUSETTS

One morning, Mouse was woken up by a heavy
CLONK! outside her front door. *Whatever's that?*
Mouse thought. She hopped out of bed, opened
the door, and looked outside. In front of her was
an ENORMOUS package. It was wrapped in brown
paper and tied with string.
CONSTRUCTION KIT was stamped on the
front, and a pink card hung from the side.
It read,

    To Mouse,
Put together the things you see,
Then climb aboard and visit me!
    Love from Rat.

    "Oooooh!" squeaked Mouse.
She nibbled through the string,
peeled off the paper, and opened
the package.

Inside was a mountain of bits and pieces—
just *waiting* to be put together.
 Mouse sniffed them and snuffled them.
 She poked them and prodded them.
"I can put these together," she said.
"NO problem."

To Mouse,
Put together the things you see,
Then climb aboard and visit me!
 Love from Rat

She was in such a hurry to begin that she *forgot* to look for
the instructions. She didn't see the sheet of paper that said,
CONSTRUCTION KIT. HOW TO PUT IT TOGETHER!

Mouse got to work.

She joined pipes here
and attached wheels there.

She twisted
and turned things.

She fiddled
and twiddled things.

She bolted bolts
and tightened nuts.

Then she stepped back to see what she'd made.
"Gosh!" said Mouse. "What *can* it be? It's a little like a bike . . .
but it isn't a bike. I think I'll call it a Biker-Riker."
She climbed on, started the engine, and set off to see Rat.

The Biker-Riker was very jumpy and very
wobbly. It jumped from wheel to wheel and kept popping
"wheelies" by mistake.

"OOOOH!" cried Mouse, hanging on tight.
"MayBE I didn't put it toGETHER riGHT."

She was tottering along on one wheel, when
she met Badger.

"Well, hello there, Mouse," growled Badger,
peering over the top of her glasses. "What is
that very peculiar *thing* you're riding?"

"It's a Biker-Riker," squeaked Mouse.
"A present from Rat. I put it together, but I
don't think it's right. It's very jumpy and
very wobbly."

"Do you have the instructions?" asked Badger.

"No," said Mouse. "Can you help?"

Badger polished her glasses and blinked at
the Biker-Riker. "Well now," she mumbled.
"Let's see. Hmmmmmm."
Then she looked up and
said, "I can fix this.
NO problem."

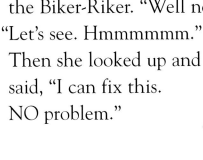

Badger unscrewed the screws and unbolted the bolts.

She shifted and shoved things.

She changed and rearranged things.

She reset the pipes and the wheels.

Then she stepped back to see what she'd made.

"Ahhh," said Badger. "What *can* it be? It's like a car . . . but it isn't a car. I think I'll call it a Jaloppy-Doppy."

"Come on," said Mouse. "Let's go to Rat's."

Mouse and Badger climbed into the Jaloppy-Doppy and set off to see Rat.

The Jaloppy-Doppy was very bumpy and very rattly, and not at all comfortable.

"May-be," said Badger, bouncing up and down, "I did-n't put it to-ge-ther ri-ght."

They were juddering along a riverbank, when they met Otter.

"Hey!" grinned Otter. "What the heck is that?"

"It's a Jaloppy-Doppy," snorted Badger.

"Rat sent it to Mouse. I put it together, but I don't think it's right. It's very bumpy and very rattly."

"Got the instructions?" asked Otter.

"Sadly, no," said Badger. "Can you help?"

Otter dived into the Jaloppy-Doppy and rolled out again. She climbed up the front and slid down the back.

"I can fix this," said Otter. "NO problem."

She squeezed underneath and unbolted the bolts.

She switched things and swapped things.

She flipped things and flopped things.

She moved all the wheels and she rebuilt the pipes.

Then she stepped back to see what she'd made.

"Wow!" barked Otter. "What *can* it be? It's a little like a boat . . . but it isn't a boat. I'm gonna call it a Boater-Roater."

"Come on," said Mouse and Badger. "Let's go to Rat's."

Mouse, Badger, and Otter pushed the Boater-Roater onto the river. They jumped in and set off to see Rat.

The Boater-Roater kept rocking and rolling, and letting in lots of water.

"*Geeeee*," said Otter, swaying to and fro.

"May*beeeeee* I didn't put it toge*eeeeee*ther ri*iiiii*ght."

They were sailing around a bend, when they met Shrew.

"Hi!" piped Shrew. "What's that?"

"It's a Boater-Roater," said Otter. "Rat sent it to Mouse. I put it together, but I don't think it's right. It keeps rocking and rolling."

"Do you have the instructions?" asked Shrew.

"No," said Otter. "Can you help?"

Shrew jumped into the Boater-Roater and scampered all over it. She peeped into corners, peered through pipes, and peeked around poles. Then . . . she found something.

"YES!" said Shrew.
"I can fix this.
NO problem."

They pulled the Boater-Roater onto the riverbank.

Shrew didn't

She *completely dismantled* the Boater-Roater.

And peering down

"Pass me this!" she ordered Mouse.

"Pass me that!" she snapped at Badger.

"Give me those!" she said to Otter.

switch things,   or swap things,   or flip things,   or flop things.

at a sheet of paper, she laid all the pieces in rows on the grass.

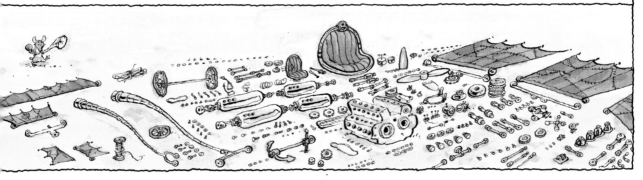

Then piece by piece and nut by bolt, she built a wonderful . . .

AIRPLANE!

"How did you do it?" asked Mouse, Badger, and Otter.

"Easy!" laughed Shrew. "I followed the instructions!"
And she waved the sheet of paper that said,

CONSTRUCTION KIT.
HOW TO PUT IT TOGETHER!

"Well, I'll be!" said the others. "Come on, let's go
to Rat's."

So Mouse, Badger, Otter, and Shrew climbed into the
airplane and set off to see Rat.

They raced across the grass and rose into the air.

"*Yoo-reeka!*" squeaked Mouse.

"*Yowler-rowler!*" growled Badger.

"*Bonanza!*" barked Otter.

"*Yazoo!*" piped Shrew.

The airplane didn't jump or wobble,
or bump or rattle, or rock or roll. It just flew
smoothly through the sky all the way to Rat's.

They landed the plane and climbed out.

"Look!" said Mouse. "There are balloons on Rat's door. She must be having a party."

The door swung open and out jumped Rat.

"HAPPY BIRTHDAY, MOUSE!" said Rat.

"Happy birthday," said Badger and Otter and Shrew.

"Did you forget? It's your birthday! We're having a party."

"My birthday?" said Mouse. "Well, I never!"

"I see you got the airplane," said Rat. "Did you have any trouble putting it together?"

Mouse winked at Badger. Otter winked at Shrew.
"NO problem," they said.

About this book

In *No Problem*, Mouse, Badger, and Otter use their knowledge of different machines (a bike, a boat, a car) to fit the shapes of the construction kit together. They do this by trial and error—estimating, thinking, and adjusting parts. When they compare the machines they've built to the ones they know, they realize that they haven't put the pieces together correctly.

Shrew has a different, more systematic way. She follows the instructions, lays out the pieces of the kit, and then fits them together in order. The construction kit seems to pose a big problem, but each animal breaks it down into manageable parts and solves it in a different way.

At this stage in their math development, the particular way children solve a problem is less important than their willingness to try different ways and to share and learn from their experiments. As they gain confidence, they will learn to choose more efficient, appropriate ways to tackle problems.

Notes for parents

Looking at the shape and size of packages gives us an idea of what's inside. Use the picture of the package at the beginning of the story to talk about what Mouse's present could—and couldn't—be. Imagining different possibilities is a good way to help children learn about shapes.

Everyday activities, like getting dressed, can show children that it's helpful to do things in a particular order.

In *No Problem*, Shrew checks off the pieces of the construction kit on a list. Whenever you talk about what they need to take on an outing, you are encouraging children to check things and organize their thoughts and ideas.

The animals in the story watch each other solving a problem in different ways. Children often see you tackling everyday tasks, and it can be helpful to them to explain what you're doing as you go along.

If you put it on its side, I can fit the nut.

Many children enjoy doing jigsaw puzzles. A jigsaw is a problem to be solved, and children often develop their own ways of approaching it. They may do the edges first, sort the pieces by color, or look at the picture to get an idea of the whole. You can sometimes help by pointing out that shapes look different when seen from different angles.

What if you turn it around?

It fits!

In the story, the animals look at the different shapes
and decide how to fit them together.
Here are some useful mathematical words
for talking about making things:

long	solid	slide	over	triangle
short	hollow	roll	through	cube
wide	curved	turn	inside	cone
narrow	flat	fit	same	hexagon
thick	round	match	way	edge
thin	straight	flip	opposite	corner

Like the animals in the book, children might enjoy
making their own version of a fantastic machine.
They could use cardboard boxes or construction toys.

Math Together

The **Math Together** program is divided into two sets—Yellow Books (ages 3+) and Green Books (ages 5+). There are six books in each set, helping children learn math through stories, rhymes, games, and puzzles.

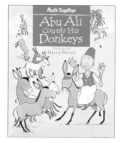